Curious George
Stories to Share

Margret *and* H. A. Rey

Houghton Mifflin Harcourt
Boston   New York

Contents

MARGRET & H.A. REY'S
Curious George
and the Firefighters

Illustrated in the style of H. A. Rey by Anna Grossnickle Hines

Houghton Mifflin Harcourt
Boston   New York

This is George.
He was a good little monkey and always very curious.
Today George and his friend the man with the yellow hat
joined Mrs. Gray and her class on their field trip to the fire station.

The Fire Chief was waiting for them right next to a big red fire truck. "Welcome!" he said, and he led everyone upstairs to begin their tour.

There was a kitchen with a big table, and there were snacks for everyone. The Fire Chief told them all about being a firefighter. George tried hard to pay attention, but there were so many things for a little monkey to explore. Like that shiny silver pole in the corner . . .

Where did that pole go? George was curious.

Why, it went back downstairs! There was the great big fire truck. There was a map of the city. And there was a whole wall full of coats and hats and big black boots!

George had an idea.
First he stepped into a
pair of boots.

Next, he picked out a helmet.

And, finally, George put on a jacket.
He was a firefighter!

Suddenly . . . *BRRRIINNGG!*

The firefighters all rushed in.

"This is not my helmet!" said one.

"My boots are too big!" said another.

"Hurry! Hurry!" called the Fire Chief. A bright red light on the map of the city told him just where the fire was. There was no time to waste!

One by one, the firefighters jumped into the fire truck.

And so did George.

The fire truck with
all the firefighters sped
out of the firehouse.
  And so did George!
  The siren screamed and the lights flashed.

The truck turned right. Then it turned left.
  WHOO WHOO WHOO went the whistle,
  and George held on tight.

And just like that the fire truck and all the firefighters pulled up to a pizza parlor on Main Street. Smoke was coming out a window in the back and a crowd was gathering in the street.

"Thank goodness you're here!" cried the cook.

The firefighters rushed off the truck and started
unwinding their hoses. They knew just what to do.
And George was ready to help.
He climbed up on the hose reel . . .

One of the firefighters saw George trying to help, and he
took George by the arm and led him out of the way.

"A fire is no place for a monkey!" he said to George. "You stay here
where it's safe."

George felt terrible.

George sat on the bench and looked around.
Next to him on the ground was a bucket
full of balls. George reached in and took
one out. It fit in his hand just
right, like the apple
he'd had for a snack.

A little girl was watching
George. He tried to give her the
ball, but she was too frightened.

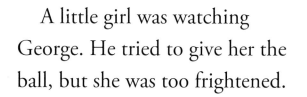

George took
another ball.

And another.
   "Look," a boy said.
"That monkey is juggling!"

The boy took a ball from the cage and
tossed it to George, but it went too high.

George climbed up onto the
fire truck to get it.

Now George had four balls to juggle. He threw the balls higher and higher. He juggled with his hands. He juggled with his feet. He could do all kinds of tricks!

The boy threw another ball to George. George threw a ball back to the boy. The little girl reached down and picked up a ball, too. Soon all the children were throwing and catching, back and forth.

The Fire Chief came to tell everyone that the fire was out. Just then, the little girl laughed and said, "Look, Mommy—a fire monkey!"

"Hey!" called the Fire Chief. "What are you doing up there?"

"What a wonderful idea," the little girl's mother said to the Fire Chief. "Bringing this brave little monkey to help children when they're frightened."

"Oh," the Fire Chief said. "Well, er, thank you."

Before long the fire truck was back at the fire house, where a familiar voice called, "George!" It was the man with the yellow hat.

"This little monkey had quite an adventure," said one of the firefighters.

"Is everyone all right?" asked Mrs. Gray.

"Yes, it was just a small fire," said the Fire Chief.
"And George was a big help."
   Now the field trip was coming to an end.
   But there was one more treat in store . . .

All the children got to take a ride around the neighborhood on the shiny red fire truck, and they each got their very own fire helmet. Even George! And it was just the right size for a brave little monkey.

MARGRET & H. A. REY'S
Curious George
at the Aquarium

by R. P. Anderson

Illustrated in the style of H. A. Rey by Anna Grossnickle Hines

Houghton Mifflin Harcourt
Boston   New York

This is George.

He was a good little monkey and always very curious.

Today George and the man with the yellow hat were visiting the aquarium.

"George," said the man, "please wait here while I buy the tickets."

George tried to wait, but he was so excited! What was inside?

28

He wanted to look over the walls, but they were too high.

Just then, he heard a *SPLASH!* and a *WHOOSH!* Water flew high into the air. People cheered. What could that be? George was curious.

He hopped over the gate into the aquarium. How surprised he was!

Swimming right in front of George were two beluga whales!
The mother and baby beluga whale swam right past him.

And not far away was a family of sea lions, diving and splashing. What fun!

George noticed people walking toward a big door—could there be more to see? He followed the crowd.

Now where was he? It was darker
inside and there were fish everywhere!
George did not know where to look first.

In one tank there were sharp-toothed piranhas,

in another tank there were sea horses,

and in another tank there was a large red octopus!

George saw a group of children across the room. An aquarium staff member was pointing to different sea creatures. "This is a starfish, this is a clam, and this is an urchin."

Nearby, there was a long, low, colorful tank. It was perfect for touching!

George was curious. As he reached his hand into the water, a large crab came scuttling out from under a rock and right toward his finger!

Snap!

Ouch!

Poor George. He did not like this exhibit.

DO NOT TOUCH

George slipped out a door into the sunlight. But, oh! What was going on here?

George saw fat, funny-looking black and white fish flying under the water. As he watched they flew up out of the water. What kind of fish does that, and where did they go? George wondered.

George climbed up and into their exhibit.

They were not fish at all, but penguins, of course!

George hopped like a penguin,

flapped his wings like a penguin,

and waddled like a penguin.

A crowd gathered and laughed.
But when he slid on his belly like a penguin . . .

The aquarium staff stopped by to check on the penguins.

"A monkey! In the penguin exhibit?"

George opened a door to escape, but instead . . . all the penguins ran out! Penguins, penguins everywhere!

The staff was angry at George. How could they catch all the penguins?

In all the excitement nobody noticed the penguin chick falling into the water! No one but George.

The baby penguin hadn't learned to swim yet. As only a monkey
can, George scaled the rope hanging over the beluga tank and swung
over the water, saving the chick.

The director of the aquarium and the man with the yellow hat heard the commotion and came running.

"That monkey helped the baby penguin," said a boy in the crowd.

"No one else could have saved him," said a girl.

The director thanked George for his help and made him an honorary staff member of the aquarium.

George said goodbye to his new penguin friends. He could not wait to come back to the aquarium and visit them again!

MARGRET & H.A. REY'S
Curious George's
Dinosaur Discovery

Written by Catherine Hapka

Illustrated in the style of H. A. Rey by Anna Grossnickle Hines

Houghton Mifflin Harcourt
Boston   New York

This is George.

He was a good little monkey and always very curious.

George loved to go places with his friend the man with the yellow hat. One of their favorite places to visit was the Dinosaur Museum.

"Today is a special day," George's friend said. "We are going to do something very interesting!"

George was curious. What could be more interesting than a trip to the Dinosaur Museum?

The man with the yellow hat led the way through the museum. George wanted to stop and look at the dinosaur bones. But his friend kept going, so George kept following.

Finally they walked right out the back door!

A van was waiting for them outside. "Climb in, George," said the man with the yellow hat.

George looked out the window as the van drove off. Where could they be going?

At last, the van reached a rocky quarry. Dozens of people were there. Some were digging with shovels. Others were using pickaxes or other kinds of tools.

"Surprise!" George's friend said. "We're going to help the museum scientists dig for dinosaur bones!"

George was curious. Were there really dinosaurs buried in the quarry? He ran over for a better look. "Hello," said a friendly scientist. "Are you here to help with the dig?"

George watched the
scientist work. She dug up
some dirt and put it into
her sifting pan.

It took a long time to sift it.
And in the end—no dinosaur
bones!

"Oh, well," she said. "Time
to try again!"

But the next pan was empty, too. So was the next one. And the one after that.

George yawned. So far digging for dinosaurs was not as exciting as he'd expected.

George was curious. Could he help to find dinosaur bones?

He found a spare shovel lying nearby. He dug and dug.
But he didn't find any dinosaurs.

When he climbed out of his hole, George spotted another scientist. He was dusting something with a small brush.

"Oh, well," the scientist said. "It's not a bone. Just a rock."

George wanted to help. He picked up
a brush and went to work.

But it turns out that monkeys are
not very good at dusting!

As he hurried away from the cloud of dust, George bumped into a wheelbarrow. Maybe there were dinosaur bones in it!

He climbed up to look inside. But the wheelbarrow was awfully tippy . . .

CRASH!

George, the wheelbarrow, and a whole lot of dirt went flying.
"Hey!" someone cried. "What's that monkey doing?"

George scampered away, straight up the cliff. Monkeys are good at climbing, so George kept going — higher and higher.

When he got to the top, he accidentally knocked a stone over the edge.

That stone hit another stone . . .

which hit another stone . . .

and another . . .

Oh, no! It was a rockslide!

The man with the yellow hat
called for George to come down.
George wanted to climb down,
but he was afraid the scientists
would be angry with him.

But the scientists didn't
look angry.

"Look!" one cried,
pointing. "Look what that
monkey just uncovered!"

George could hardly believe what he saw. Dinosaur bones!

After that, the dinosaur dig was even more fun. George helped the scientists dig . . .

and sift . . .

and dust . . .

and take photographs of
the bones he had found.

And the next time he and the man with the yellow hat visited the Dinosaur Museum, George got to see HIS dinosaur on display!

MARGRET & H. A. REY'S
Curious George's
First Day of School

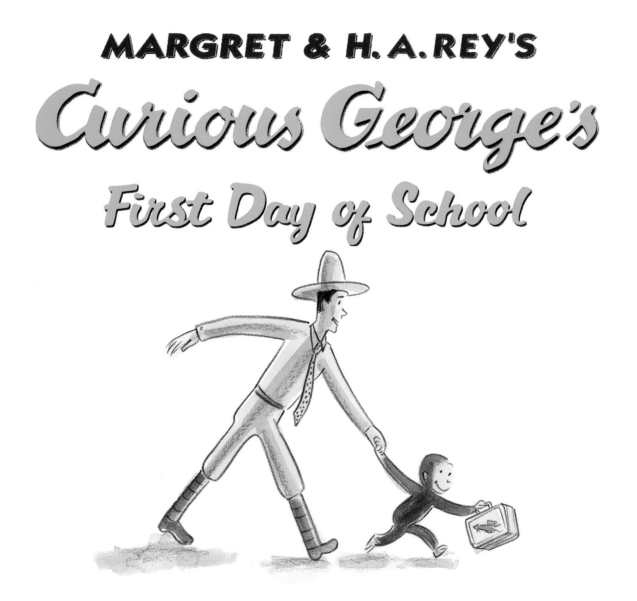

Illustrated in the style of H. A. Rey by Anna Grossnickle Hines

Houghton Mifflin Harcourt
Boston   New York

This is George.

He was a good little monkey and always very curious.

Today George was so excited, he could barely eat his breakfast. "You have a big day ahead of you, George," said his friend the man with the yellow hat.

It *was* a big day for George. It was the first day of school, and he had been invited to be a special helper.

George and his friend walked together to the schoolyard. Some of the children were nervous, but George could not wait for the fun to begin.

In the classroom George's friend introduced him to Mr. Apple. "Thank you for inviting George to school today," the man with the yellow hat said to the teacher. Then he waved goodbye. "Have a good day, George. I'll be back to pick you up after school."

The children were excited to have a monkey in class. "George is going to be our special helper," Mr. Apple told them.

And what a helper he was! At story time George held the book.

At math time the children could count on George.

And at recess George made sure
everyone had a ball . . .

and a well-balanced snack.

After lunch Mr. Apple got out paints and brushes. George saw red, yellow, and blue paint. Three colors were not very many. George was curious. Could he help make more colors?

First George mixed red and blue to make . . .

purple.

Next George mixed red and yellow to make . . .

orange.

Then George mixed
yellow and blue to make . . .

green.

Finally George mixed all
the colors to make . . .

. . . a big mess!

The children thought the mess was funny. But Mr. Apple did not.

"Oh, dear," he said. "We are going to need something to clean this up. Everyone please sit quietly while I look."

George did not mean to make such a mess and he certainly did not want to sit quietly. He wanted to help—it was his job, after all. George had an idea.

In the
hallway
George
found
a closet.
In the
closet
he found
a bucket.
In the bucket
he found just
what he needed . . .

87

A mop!

George was on his way back to the classroom when he heard somebody yell.

"Stop! Stop! What are you doing with my mop?" The janitor ran after George.

"Stop! Stop! No running in the halls!" The principal ran after the janitor.

But George was going too fast to stop. He grabbed the doorway and swung inside, and . . .

S
P
L
O
S
H
!

The bucket tipped,
the mop dropped,
and George slid
across the floor.

Now the mess was even bigger.

Mr. Apple looked surprised. The principal frowned. The janitor just shook his head.

And George—poor George. He felt terrible. Maybe he was not such a good helper after all.

The children felt terrible too. They did not like to see
George looking so sad. They thought he was a great helper.
Now they wanted to help him.

So the children all lent a hand (and some feet).

And before anyone knew it, the mess was gone!

"That little monkey sure is helpful," the janitor said.

"It looks like Mr. Apple has a whole class full of helpers," the principal added.

At the end of the day, when George's friend arrived to pick him up, Mr. Apple said, "Thank you for all of your help, George. We hope you will come help us again."

The children cheered. They hoped George would come again too.

George waved goodbye to his new friends. What a great day it had been! He could not wait to come back to school.

MARGRET & H.A. REY'S
Curious George
and the Pizza Party

Written by Cynthia Platt
Illustrated in the style of H. A. Rey by Mary O'Keefe Young

Houghton Mifflin Harcourt
Boston   New York

George was a good little monkey and always very curious. Today, he wasn't just curious—he was excited. So excited, in fact, that he was turning flips and standing on his head!

A little girl in George's building had invited him to her pizza party. George had never been to a pizza party before, but he loved parties and he loved pizza, so he knew it had to be good.

"George, it's time for the pizza party," said the man with the yellow hat.

"Have fun—and remember to be on your best behavior!"

George got to the party in perfect time!

"Hi, George," called out the little girl. But oh, what was all of this? The children were wearing puffy white chef's hats and checkered aprons.

George got a hat and an apron, too! The best was yet to come. They weren't just going to eat pizza. They were going to make it, too.

"Everyone will get a piece of pizza dough to roll out and make a special pizza," explained the girl's mother. There were many little lumps of dough.

"But first, let's play some games!" she said.

Everyone went into the living room to play pin the pepperoni on the pizza. Everyone, that is, except George. He was curious about those pieces of dough.

George thought and thought. If lots of little pieces of dough were good, maybe one huge one would be even better.

He gathered the lumps of dough together and
squished and squashed them until they became the
very biggest piece of dough he'd ever seen. What fun!
Maybe rolling it out would be even more fun!

George poured flour out on the table, and he rolled and rolled and rolled the dough with a rolling pin.

It was messy work! First he bumped over one of the chairs.

Crash!

Then he knocked over the sack of flour. *Thump!*

The flour looked like snow lying on the floor of the kitchen.
George liked snow, though, so he didn't mind at all.
Soon he had gotten the dough nice and thin.

But the thinner it got, the farther it spread out.
Before he knew it, the dough covered the
table . . . then the chairs . . . and then George.

Without the flour, it started to stick to everything—including George!
George stopped to think.

Maybe the dough was better off in small pieces after all.

George got a pair of scissors and began cutting
up the dough into lots of different shapes.
He thought everyone would be pleased.

"George! What have you done to the kitchen?"
The little girl's mother didn't look very happy.
"I think it's time for you to go home now."
    How surprised and sad George was.

Just then, the children burst into the kitchen
and saw the mess that George had made.

"George, what happened?" asked one boy.
The other children looked at the shapes George
had made with wide eyes.

"Wow, George! I've never seen pizza dough like
that before," said the little girl, smiling.

"Well," said her mother, "if you can clean up this mess quickly, George, I suppose you can still stay to make pizza."

The children all helped George clean the kitchen.
He was lucky to have so many good friends.

   As they worked, they talked about the pizza!
 "I'm going to make a pizza that looks like a star,"
said one little boy.

   "And I'm going to make one that looks like
a house!" said a girl.

115

Once the kitchen was clean, the real fun began!
All of the children picked out perfect pieces of
dough and got to work.

They spooned on tomato sauce and sprinkled on cheese.
They added lots of vegetables and pepperoni.

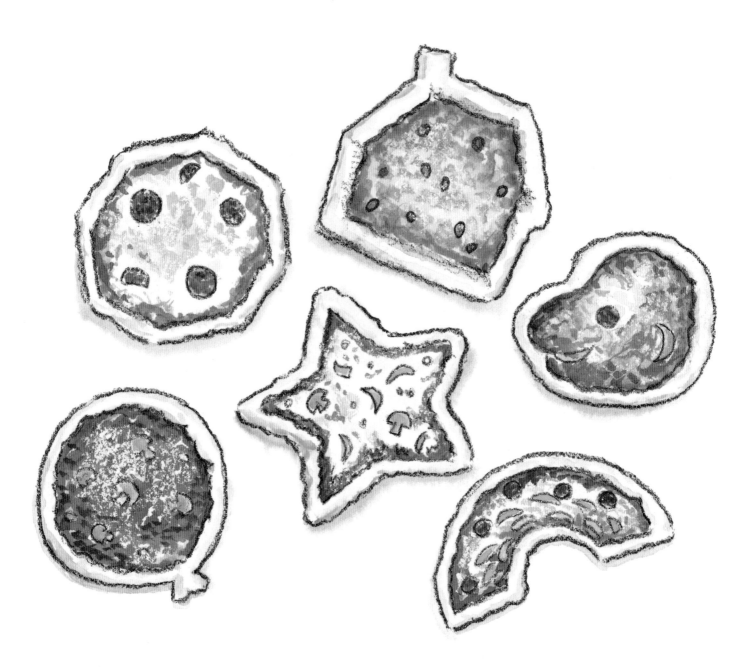

The pizzas looked wonderful! One looked like a rainbow, another like a stop sign, and still another like a balloon. There was even a pizza that looked curiously like George!

"Well, George," said the little girl's mother, "the pizzas taste great, and thanks to you, they look wonderful, too!"

Everyone agreed. It was the best pizza anyone had ever seen—or tasted!

For the second time that day, George was so
happy that he turned flips and stood on his head.

Of course, it was a little harder to turn flips with so
much pizza in his belly. But George didn't mind.
It had been a wonderful pizza party!

MARGRET & H.A.REY'S

Curious George
at the Baseball Game

Written by Laura Driscoll

Illustrated in the style of H. A. Rey by Anna Grossnickle Hines

Houghton Mifflin Harcourt
Boston   New York

This is George.

He was a good little monkey and always very curious.

Today George and the man with the yellow hat were going to the ballpark to watch a baseball game. George couldn't wait to see what it would be like.

At the baseball stadium, the man with the yellow hat introduced George to his friend, the head coach of the Mudville Miners. He had arranged for George to watch the game from the dugout. What a treat! George got a Miners cap to wear. Then he sat on the bench with the players. He felt just like part of the team!

The players cheered a Miners home run. George cheered, too.

The players groaned at a Miners strikeout. George groaned, too.

Then George noticed one of the Miners coaches making funny motions with his hands. He touched his cap. He pinched his nose. He dusted off his shoulder.

Hmm, thought George. Maybe this was another way to cheer on the team.

So George made some hand
motions, too. He tugged at his ear.

He rubbed his tummy.

He scratched his chin.

Just then, a Miners player got tagged out at second base. The player pointed at George. "That monkey!" he said. "He distracted me with his funny signs."

Oops! The coach had been giving directions to the base runner. George's hand signals had taken his mind off the play. Poor George! He had only been trying to be part of the team. Instead the Miners had lost a chance to score.

George watched the rest of the game from a stadium seat. Or at least he *tried* to watch the game. There was so much going on around him.

There was food for sale.

There were shouting fans.

There was a woman holding a big camera . . .

The woman pointed her camera at some fans. And look! Those fans waved out from the huge screen on the ballpark scoreboard.

George had never been on TV before. He was very curious. What would it be like to see himself on the big screen?

He soon learned the answer: it was exciting!

The scoreboard reads:

2 BALL 0 STRIKE 1 OUT

MINERS	0	0	1	2
ROCKETS	0	1	0	

George liked seeing
himself on the screen.

"Hey, you!" shouted the
camerawoman. "Cut that out!"

Uh-oh! George had gotten a little carried away. He ran off, with the angry camerawoman hot on his heels.

In the busy stadium breezeway, George hid behind a popcorn cart. He waited for the camerawoman to pass by.

Just then, George heard a noise behind him. It was a quiet little noise—like a sigh, or a sniff. What could have made that noise? George wondered.

George turned. There, behind the cart, was a little boy, crying. George wanted to help. He crept out of his hiding place and over to the boy.

"Ah-ha! There you are!" shouted the camerawoman, spotting George. Then the camerawoman noticed the teary-eyed boy. She seemed to forget that she was mad at George.

"I'm lost," the boy said. "I can't find my dad."

If only there were a way to let the boy's dad know where he was. But there *was* a way! The camerawoman aimed her lens at the little boy, and . . .

there he was on the big screen for everyone to see—including his dad.

Within minutes, the boy and his father were together again and the man with the yellow hat had come to find George.

"I can't thank you enough," the boy's father said to the camerawoman.

The camerawoman shrugged. "Don't thank me," she said. She patted George on the back. "It was this little fellow who found your son."

George was the star of the day.

MARGRET & H.A.REY'S
Curious George
at the Parade

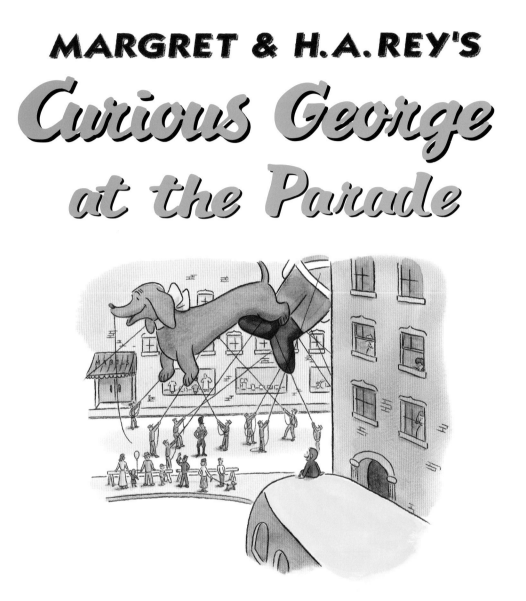

Illustrated in the style of H. A. Rey by Vipah Interactive

Houghton Mifflin Harcourt
Boston   New York

This is George.

He was a good little monkey and always very curious.

Today George and his friend, the man with the yellow hat, were in the city for the big holiday parade.

They found a place in the crowd, but an announcement had just been made.

"The parade may not start for a while, George," the man said. "The wind is too strong for the big balloons. Let's go in this department store while we wait."

George and his friend looked around the store as they waited for
the wind to settle down. Suddenly, something strange caught George's
eye. What could it be? He was curious.

But when George looked out the window,

he didn't see anything strange. He saw the parade! He saw floats, clowns, and jugglers, and a band standing in straight rows.
Then George thought he saw an elephant eating a treat.

That made George hungry. (It had been a long time since breakfast.) Now he could think only of finding a snack.

Why, here was a treat just like what he ate in the jungle: fresh nuts—right off the tree!

George was lucky to be a monkey . . .

he simply climbed out the window and jumped into the tree!

Then he pulled and pulled. But the nuts would not come off the tree. They were not so fresh after all. In fact, they were not even real. But George did not know that.

He pulled harder and harder. The tree began to sway . . .

Suddenly, there was a loud *SNAP!*

Then, *CRASH!*
Down came the tree.
Down came George.
And down came all the nuts!

Luckily, George was not hurt. But still he did not have a snack. He raced after the nuts. He chased them around the elephant and under the clown, then in and out of the band's straight rows. "My perfect rows!" the bandleader cried. "You've ruined my perfect rows!"

The bandleader raced after George. He chased him down the street and around the corner, but he was not quick enough.

Where was George?

Soon the bandleader tired of searching and went back to straighten his rows. He did not know where the little monkey had gone — George was nowhere to be found.

George was not sure where he had gone either — and the nuts were nowhere to be found. After all that, George had lost his snack. After all that, George had lost his way. Now how would he get back to the department store and back to the man with the yellow hat?

Just then a bus was stopping at the corner. George liked to ride the bus. Maybe it could take him back to his friend. Quickly, he hopped on the bus and away they went.

From his seat up on top,
George could see everything.
The bus rounded a corner.
Here was something familiar!

But something was wrong. Two balloons had drifted off course—
their ropes were tangled. The parade helpers were trying to fix them
and a crowd gathered to watch. As the bus came to a stop, someone

162

yelled, "Catch that monkey! He's ruined our parade!" It was the bandleader, and he was pointing right at George!

George did not want to be caught, but there was no way for him to get down. There was only one way to go . . .

George grabbed a rope and went UP!

Up, up he climbed, higher and higher. He was a little frightened, but he held on tight. Then he heard someone call: "GEORGE!" It was the man with the yellow hat! George was happy to find his friend. The man was happy, too.

George swung from one rope to another. Now he felt like he was in the jungle swinging from vine to vine.

"Look," someone shouted from below. "The little monkey is fixing the balloons!"

Then George swung safely into the arms of the man with the yellow hat! The crowd below cheered—the ropes were no longer tangled!

When George and his friend arrived back on the sidewalk, it was time to start the parade.

The bandleader was no longer angry—George was a hero! Even
the mayor came to meet George. "I hear you created quite a stir,
George," he said. "But at last everything is in order. Would you like
to ride with me in the parade?"

Soon the balloons started moving, the music started playing, and the band marched down the street in straight rows.

And there, leading the whole parade, was Curious George.

MARGRET & H.A.REY'S
Curious George Plants a Tree

Written by Monica Perez
Illustrated in the style of H. A. Rey by Anna Grossnickle Hines

Houghton Mifflin Harcourt
Boston   New York

George was a good little monkey and always very curious. Today was a good day to be curious. The man with the yellow hat was taking George to the Science Museum.

The museum was one of George's favorite places. There was always something new to see and interesting to learn.

Often there was a special exhibit. George wanted to know what it was today, but first he had to make his favorite museum stops:

the rocket room,

the mirror maze,

and the butterfly space.

Finally, George and his friend made it to the special exhibits room.

The sign read HOW YOU CAN TAKE CARE OF OUR PLANET.

George learned many things:

how all people, animals, plants, air, and water on the planet make up the environment,
how trees help keep the air clean,
and how people can help protect the environment from pollution and too much trash.

George had a great time and didn't get into any of his usual mischief.

As he and his friend were leaving,
they bumped into the museum director.

Dr. Lee looked happy to see him.

"How is my best monkey visitor?" Dr. Lee asked George. "I'm so glad I ran into you. I wanted to tell you that we're having a Green Day rally tomorrow at the park."

George was curious—whatever a rally was, he was sure that the park was a good place to do it.

"We're going to plant a truckload of trees and collect used paper for recycling," Dr. Lee explained. "We didn't have much time to advertise, but we need lots of volunteers. How would you like to help out?"

There was nothing that George liked better than to help.

"What a great idea!" the man agreed. "We'll be there."

That night George was ready to do his part for the recycling drive. He gathered every newspaper in the house. He stacked old mail on top of the papers. He piled empty cardboard boxes and food cartons on top of that. What a heap!

What more could he add? George scratched his head.
Then he took several books off his bedroom shelf.

Just as George was about to add them to his recycling pile, someone lifted the books out of his hands.

"Not so fast, George," the man said. "These books are made of paper all right, but you can read and enjoy them many times. And when you're done, you can donate them to other kids or your library. Reusing is just as important as recycling."

The next morning
George and his friend set
out for the park with their
wagon of neatly stacked paper.
Suddenly the man stopped and said,
"I forgot my gardening gloves! Go on
without me, George. I'll be there soon."

As George walked down the street, he spotted
several newspapers lying about on his neighbors' front
stoops. George had an idea. He had lots of room in his
wagon. He could recycle all those newspapers.

And the newspapers were not the only things he could recycle. He noticed a stack of paper cups sitting on a table under a tree. Into the wagon they went!

So did a pile of magazines.

And a heap of papers someone left on the sidewalk.

George was happy with his great load. At the park, he found Dr. Lee standing under a big banner.

"Good morning, George," Dr. Lee said. "I'm so glad you came and brought all your friends. We need lots of help to get the job done."

George turned around. He was surprised to see
so many faces, but they did not look very helpful.
They looked angry!

The man with the yellow hat arrived just in time. He explained to their neighbors that George was gathering paper for a good cause. They were no longer mad. They even stayed to help plant the trees.

191

"George, you saved our Green Day!" Dr. Lee said, with gratitude. "These trees will provide fresher air. And each summer we'll have more shade, which means we'll use less water to keep the grass green. Thank you."

Being a monkey, George had known all along how important trees were.

Living Green

Here are some simple everyday things that you and your family can do to conserve energy and resources:

1. Use both sides of your paper.
2. Make your own playthings out of cardboard boxes and paper towel rolls.
3. Talk to your teacher about classroom recycling.
4. Donate your gently used books to a library.
5. Donate your gently used clothing to a charity.
6. At mealtimes, don't take more food than you can finish.
7. Turn off lights, air conditioning, and heat when not in use.
8. Look for the recycling symbol on packages when you shop.
9. Fill the bathtub up only halfway.
10. Turn off the faucet while brushing your teeth.
11. Ask your parents to buy rechargeable batteries.
12. Use old kitchen containers and utensils as sand and water toys.
13. Volunteer to help clean up your local park.
14. Open the curtains during the day to let the sun warm your house.
    Close the curtains at night to keep the heat in.
15. Take care of your house plants—they help purify the air.
16. Make your own birthday and holiday cards.
17. Use newspaper comics to wrap gifts.
18. If you live near your school, walk or bike instead of driving.
19. Take your own bags to the grocery store.
20. Help plant a tree and watch it grow.

Six Steps for Planting a Tree

Step 1: Dig hole.

Step 2: Remove burlap from root ball and stand tree in hole.

Step 3: Fill in dirt, tamping lightly as you go.

**Step 4: Put
stakes around tree.**

Step 5: Water.

Step 6: Mulch.